PRIVATELY FAMOUS

HANK RAMSAN

Ramsan, Hank
ISBN13 978-09746526-9-6
ISBN10 0-974-6526-9-5

Front Cover Image: Dahotski Dzmitry / Shutterstock

Printed in the United States of America.

"The Truth Does Not Bend, But Our Use Of It Allows Us To Bend Everything."   *—Susan James*

The Players of Privately Famous

The primary people and associates written of in this book are detailed within the story. Offered here are some simple descriptions based on my relationship with them. Others may have a different perspective. This is mine.

Jack Wade is first and foremost my best friend. Secondly, Jack is the President and CEO of Wade Worldwide Publishing. He is my publisher. He's tall, sandy blond hair, like mine, deep blue eyes, handsome, trim and athletic. He fits into expensive suits like a glove.

Jack married his high school sweetheart, who has helped him build his publishing business. Her law degree has come in handy when negotiating publishing contracts, especially those for international book sales and film rights.

Jack's loyalty and business expertise is beyond question, just as is his generosity. He doesn't like to discuss this, so I won't either.

Then there is Sam, also a lifelong friend. He is a friend with special skills and connections, also which I won't discuss here. He is a man of mystery, and strives to remain just that: a mystery.

And Jocy. I'm not sure about her just yet. She's petite, short dark hair, ivory skin, brown eyes, a tailored yet often casual dresser. When in business situations, she seems quite confident. Being with her one-on-one, she seems at times to be in fear and on edge.

The attraction that I feel for Jocy seems to be reciprocated. I felt myself falling hard for her, but not sure if I could trust my own feelings or her intentions, both said and unsaid.

Jocy and I met at a writers' conference we were both attending in NYC. I happened to be the main speaker and award recipient.

Was our meeting planned by others? Or was it a blessed accident?

Hank Ramsan

ONE

The annual meeting of The Writers and Publishers Conference was held at the St. Regis in New York City. This was a perfect location for artists of all venues. It was near Fifth Avenue, the Museum of Modern Art, The Rockefeller Center, Grand Central, Central Park, the subway and Trump Tower.

Jack Wade, President and CEO of Wade Worldwide Publishing hosted this year's event. A wide variety of artists from writers to painters to sculptors eagerly anticipated this year's main speaker. The reason? Well, the main speaker was *me*, Hank Ramsan. It was known that I had a unique way of reaching my level of success, and many were excited to hear my *how-I-did-it* story. The challenge for me, how much of it was I going to *tell* at this stage.

Seated next to me, Jack Wade leaned from his chair to retrieve a fallen napkin. That's when I saw her. Startled by her beauty, my trance was only broken when Jack turned to me and said, "Boy, what are your eyes locked on?"

Jack was my best friend, and one of my contacts in high places. We'd been friends since childhood. Blue eyed, sandy-blond haired like mine, we could almost pass for brothers. It had been Jack who offered me the deal of a lifetime, the deal for my manuscript *Paperback Writer.* This dinner was in honor of the worldwide sales and its writer, me, Hank Ramsan.

"Who's that?" Was my immediate response as I tried nonchalantly to point my head in *her* direction.

Jack turned to see who had me in a trance, and immediately knew without question who I was salivating over. "That's Jocy. Everyone knows her. And everyone loves her. Oh and Hank, everyone wants to be with her, including the fellow standing at her side."

Her petite figure was perfection. Her short, lustrous dark hair framed a delicate face of the purest ivory.

Jack broke my concentration saying, "She's some kind of art dealer and horse enthusiast. As you can imagine, she has many wealthy contacts. Many of them are in publishing."

"Ok," I said, barely paying attention. Jocy had the most beautiful brown eyes. I slowly turned to my friend. "Jack, do you know if they're together...you know *together*, together?"

"I don't know for sure, but I've seen them at several events. She's not married to him, if that's what you really want to know."

Scooting my chair from the table I said, "Ok, then. I know you'll excuse me while I see if I can find a way to introduce myself."

"Don't forget Hank, you are the guest of honor here this evening and you have a speech to make. Don't forget that Hank!" Jack was trying to convey his concern casually, but I got the message.

"I'll be back in time, with or without the introduction." But I *knew* I would get one.

Two

For what now seemed like too long, I'd been spending most of my time in my writing loft simply writing and not romancing anyone, not even a stone. It hadn't seemed that important, or maybe it was that someone that important hadn't caught my eye, until now.

But there was no mistake. I had to meet this girl, and I had to meet her now. I was having one of my Ray Bradbury moments, where the rush was worth the chase.

Meeting this Jocy person, so that it seemed innocent was not going to be easy. I had to hurry, but not appear hurried.

And then my moment came like a gift on a golden chocolate platter.

Her date noticed me over by the dessert table, and he and Jocy came my way. "You're the guest of honor here this evening, aren't you? You're Hank Ramsan?" The questions came from the lucky man at *her* side.

"Yes, you caught me," I answered, reaching to shake his hand. "And you are...?"

"Shawn Demmon, and this is my lovely Jocy."

My ears perked up when he said, this is '*my* lovely Jocy'. It didn't set well.

Jocy reached out her dainty but firm soft hand. I felt as if I could describe every inch of her hand from that one moment of touching it.

Her skin on mine sent a torch throughout my body. It was all I could do to remain calm and professional. I hadn't been this affected, well since *never*. She smiled, and I wanted to live forever in that beautiful smile.

She glanced over the dessert table. "Everything looks delicious. What will you choose?"

I was still focused on her mouth, so inviting. She wore plum-colored lipstick. "...Something with ripe plums."

She smiled.

All of a sudden this fellow Shawn became very interested in me. He wanted to know how I was investing my publishing worth. He was one of those people who had not yet earned their personal space to ask those levels of questions and get an answer.

Jocy looked as if she'd been in this uncomfortable position before, having her boyfriend approach friends of hers about their money and investments.

I couldn't help but wonder why she was with this guy. He didn't seem to be her style. Or maybe I was a bit jealous. Maybe it was both. As I was about to answer him in a non-committal and evasive fashion, I heard my name called from the podium.

Reluctantly, I quickly excused myself from Jocy and Shawn, but not without Jocy's eyes locking with mine. Those alert brown eyes were full of questions.

That was all this blond boy needed. I was *in*.

THREE

From the podium I couldn't tell much about the audience, due to the room's large capacity and the lights in my face. I tried to search out Jocy's brown eyes and plum-colored lips. I couldn't tell where she was seated. Was she still there, or had that Shawn person taken her away? *Enough!* It was important to keep my wits about me. This was an important moment for me, and for Wade Worldwide Publishing.

The underlying theme of this speech would also be important for many who would be reading *Paperback Writer*. My future ventures and backlist books would also increase in sales momentum. I had developed and applied my own 'User Friendly Physics' to the attainment of this moment. And even though I needed to remain focused on the receipt of this honor from Jack Wade, I knew I would use these same dynamics to see where my interest with Jocy would lead.

I'm one of those writers who didn't know that writing was supposed to be what I'd do with my life and livelihood. Which means, I've kissed a lot of frog-type careers and jobs to finally land in the pond that made me happiest: Writing.

Looking back, as many of us do, there was a thread that did show itself. I wrote for my high school newspaper, but my reasons for working on the paper had nothing to do with any interest in writing. At least I didn't know it at the time. But there I was.

I also wrote a paper at the end of my college experience, which told me something about myself. But again, it didn't tell me that I was a writer. It was a good paper, and I had written it. That's what I kept noticing.

Paying attention to my own creed of 'notice what you notice' didn't take hold until some years later.

Noticing what I was noticing in this moment was my attraction to Jocy. This attraction was taking precedent over this outstanding honor that I was being given from one of the most well-respected and sought after publishing houses. The world of publishing was watching this moment. The domino effect would carry its way throughout the world in an even more expanded readership of my work. *Pay attention!*

I knew I would need to compartmentalize myself so that I would give a great acceptance speech, while being fully aware that Jocy too, would be hearing it. I needed to be better than good. I wanted to be dynamic.

FOUR

My speech was the usual type of autobiographical information, relating the path from there to here. I wanted to keep it short, concise and inspiring. Mostly short, as folks were there also to enjoy a good time. I wanted to send them out the door feeling energized and enthusiastic, and not bored.

In addition to the New Yorkers with deep pockets, there were many new writers in the room. These were writers with big hopes and dreams. They wanted their words to matter to readers.

The circle of Publishing includes aficionados of the art world. Art and writing bring a huge creative mix to any gathering, and this gathering brought me Jocy. Making sure I saw her again before she left for the evening was paramount.

FIVE

As we welcomed questions from the audience, my mind was preoccupied with Jocy leaving before we reconnected. I didn't want to miss an opportunity to speak with her again. Out of the corner of my eye, I caught a glimpse of her and Shawn standing at their table, as if preparing to go.

All of a sudden, like a flash of genius or half-witted insight, I blurted out, "Are their any art dealers in the room?"

She turned that beauty of a face towards me, and beamed. It was a beam from heaven; I know it was. It was a beam that said, "I hoped you'd find a way for us to speak again this evening." Well, that's what I told myself it meant.

The possibility there were art dealers in the room, other than Jocy, hadn't even occurred to me. Everyone's eyes were locked on me, waiting to find out what I would say next. I had nuthin'.

Jack Wade, knowing me as he did, understood what I was up to. He knew he needed to save this moment for me, before I completely embarrassed myself and Wade Worldwide Publishing.

Slowly rising from his place at the main table, Jack addressed the audience. "Hank Ramsan and I would like to announce *The Wade-Ramsan Creative Arts Consortium*."

Everyone in the room was surprised, and no one more surprised than me. I had no idea what was on his mind, or even if this had been on his mind. ...Or if he too, in spite of saving me, was also having a genius or brainless moment.

Jack and I looked at each other in both amazement and wonder. This actually sounded like a great idea. But this was his move. He had to follow up his announcement to the room. But before he had a chance to say anything, from the middle table in the room, Jocy spoke up.

She said, "I don't know what you have in mind, Jack, but I do know your reputation. I'd love to be involved!"

Jack and I looked at each other again ... trying to hide our smirks. We both knew what this was really about.

"Sold!" Came Jack's voice. "I'll get with you this week, Jocy, to discuss some ideas. But for those gathered here in this room, while I have a captive audience, I'll give you the general intention of The Wade-Ramsan Creative Arts Consortium."

Jack continued: "The creative arts have been good to both Hank and me. From the first word scratched on a piece of paper, to the bookstores and readers online and off. Among the readers are many writers. These writers come from diverse backgrounds, and often express fresh and interesting points of view. These are writers with the joy of storytelling or teaching in their hearts, and expand their thoughts and ideas to the written page. For far too many, this is where it stops. They have no avenue to propel their hearts desires out to others, simply because they don't have the commercial connections and the foundation for promoting their work. Everyone here understands the importance of promoting one's work." He kept going. All in the room could feel his passion in his words. Excitement was building like a wave ready to crest.

He said, "There is no better joy for any artist or writer than to have someone say, 'I really enjoyed what you have written. I really enjoyed gazing at your painting.' They go on to tell us what this thing we created has meant in their lives. But if there is no place to display our work, then we miss a crucial piece of a life experience: Joy and the feeling of accomplishment. Many miss the joy of what they love doing, due to the misconception of lack of resources to expand their work. There have always been plenty of resources. But these same people have had no idea how to 'get there'. This is where Hank Ramsan's User Friendly Physics, which have built his writing career and his lifestyle, will show the way. It will show the way for the many and the few."

And with this last sentence the room full of glitz and glamour, beauty and grace, stood and cheered.

All except ... *one*.

Jack broke through the thunderous applause saying, "The Wade-Ramsan Creative Arts Consortium or W-R-C-A-C will provide a place and an avenue for new writers and new artists to display their works on a national and international level."

SIX

Jack concluded, "We have some details to iron out, and will do so soon. Anyone interested or curious, please make sure that either Hank or I have your business card before you leave this evening."

While Jack was making his intentions known, I had my eyes on Jocy. Her boyfriend had his eyes on me.

When I started to move toward them, Shawn grabbed Jocy by the arm and pulled her away. I heard him mutter, "Ridiculous, giving a platform to unknown writers and artists. These resources should be entrusted to those of us who…" By then they were too far away for me to catch the conclusion of his sentence. I sighed. Shawn was clueless about how things really worked.

By then, they were out of the room. He was careful not to be too rough as to cause a scene, but it appeared she was leaving against her will.

Again, I had to wonder: what someone like Jocy was doing with someone like Shawn? Sensing there was no immediate danger, I backed off going after her. Besides, being the main attraction for the event, I needed to stay and help Jack closeout the evening.

A hundred or more exchanged business cards and an hour later, Jack and I headed to the Wade limo.

Both comfortably seated in the back, the driver rolled down the inner partition and pushed a small piece of paper through. "Mr. Ramsan, this note was left on the windshield. It's for you."

The note read: 'Stay away from Jocy.'

After handing it to Jack, he said, "Well Hank, I'll tell you what this may be about."

"I'm listening. Go on…"

"Since you spend most of your time in Virginia, you may not be aware of the underbelly of the art and publishing world. For some, the glitz and glamour come at a cost. Unfortunately for Jocy, she got caught up in both."

"But Jack, why do you know about this … this underbelly?"

"I have my ears close to the ground. That's how I know. I'm in the upper crust of entertainment and media. It's my job to know what's going on. I don't have to be a part of it to *see*."

"What have you *seen* that may involve Jocy?"

SEVEN

Jack settled back in the seat, and stretched out his long legs. He said, "Whatever is going on, Hank, you have to pretend you know nothing. If you really want to get close to Jocy, I can help, but you have to 'play along'. If we play this right, we can use the consortium to help you get to know Jocy better, and see what may be going on. Be prepared, though. We may learn some things that we really aren't supposed to know."

I said nothing.

"Are you game?"

"Of course I am Jack, whatever it takes."

"Ok, I'll set up a meeting with Jocy, just as I mentioned at the event. I'll not tell her anything about you coming along. We'll consider it a last minute change of plans, and you decided to tag along."

Jack and I went our separate ways, but not until I had him tell me about his idea for the consortium. Was this move planned, or was it by the seat of his pants?

Apparently he had wanted to do something like this for some time, but the right ideas and timing had not yet presented themselves. Getting around to discussing it with me was on his mind, but we both had been too busy to have a sit down over anything new. The event in my honor, and my foot in my mouth, allowed him to seize the day.

EIGHT

The meeting with Jocy was set.

We were to meet at The Four Seasons. Jack made arrangements for an intimate, private lunch. Jocy was open and understanding of the need for a private meeting. Financial considerations of the consortium would be discussed, and Jack wanted to be sure that nothing would be overheard and used prematurely to thwart its success. What she did not know was that I would be there.

Jack didn't want us to gather in the lobby prior to the meeting, as the three of us together would certainly get tongues wagging. He arranged for Jocy to check in with the concierge, and he would escort her to our private luncheon.

The knock on the door came. My heart leapt. I knew her beautiful warm smiling face would be behind that knock. What caused me to feel unsteady was wondering what her reaction would be to seeing me there.

Jack opened the door to greet her. They exchanged kisses on the cheek. As Jack moved to the side, she noticed me.

Her eyes met mine. She smiled. Again, my heart leapt.

I felt the corner of my own mouth turn up, the type of smile that I knew connected me to the correctness of any situation. This was a perfect moment.

Extending my right hand to shake hers, she followed suit. Jack said; "Jocy, I hope you don't mind that I invited Hank here today. He can help me represent the writing side of the consortium, I publishing and you art."

She smiled and said, "Of course I don't mind, it's an added pleasure of course."

I hoped she was being truthful, and not just polite.

With greetings out of the way, we sat down in the parlor area of the suite. While our lunch was brought in, Jack re-introduced his plan for the consortium. He provided more details about how the three of us could be more involved, as he expanded his vision. Although I was smitten with Jocy, I was also extremely interested in the success of Jack's plan for new authors. I listened attentively.

I understood my role, but was not sure how Jocy would play into this plan, other than my own personal interest in her.

Jack went on to explain how artists and authors have many things in common. One of them being, the lack of the financial resources to help them become 'discovered'. Jocy knew the money-players in the art world.

She knew how they preferred to invest their money, some in various art forms, some in horse breeding and various competitions of both. Many had invested widely in real estate properties. Jack and I knew the money-players in publishing, including some of the more highly successful writers, of which I, thanks to Wade Publishing, was one.

Our lunch table was set with fine fare. Moving over to the table, I noticed the waiter had a strange tattoo on his left hand. It was out of the ordinary because it looked like a woman's shoe. A stiletto, to be more exact.

Jack interrupted my train of thought by asking me if I was going to pull up Jocy's chair for her. As I did, the waiter left the room, and I forgot about him and the odd tattoo.

We enjoyed lunch, as well as each other's company. We ended the meeting with an agreement to get back together in a week. Each of us would bring the names of ten people that we felt we could contact concerning financial backing, and to support the consortium.

Jack suggested (as he always has my back), that I walk Jocy to her car, while he returned an important phone call.

NINE

The elevator ride down to the lobby revealed a different side of Jocy. She seemed suddenly insecure and a bit anxious. These were feelings I hadn't noticed before, and it surprised me to notice them now. There was something else going on that she was not ready to talk about.

Commenting on her sudden unease, I asked her if I made her feel uncomfortable.

She said, "No..." She was aware of our attraction, but she needed for me to understand that she was 'with someone else'.

I asked her if she meant Shawn.

She nodded yes. But I could tell there was much not being said, more that I wanted to know. Sensing I needed to help her in some way, I wondered what to say. I needed more information. Just as I was about to speak, the elevator door slid open.

My next move had to be clear and concise. I wanted to see her again, but privately. We needed to meet where we could talk and get to know one another without her feeling anxious. "Jocy, may I see you again? Soon?"

She said 'No' with her mouth, but 'yes' with her eyes. As we kissed a quick goodbye on the cheek, she quickly said, "We're being watched. Come to my art gallery at 6:30 a.m. tomorrow morning."

Although that seemed a bit early for any romance I had in mind, it seemed there was more she was willing to disclose to me. For that, it would never be too early.

I squeezed her hand in agreement, closed the door on her car and went back inside to find Jack.

TEN

Jack met me in the lobby and I told him about my brief conversation with Jocy, and about my plans to meet her early in the morning.

"Be careful, Hank," he warned. "I'm sure there is much more going on than even I know."

I nodded in agreement, as we discussed getting together after my meeting with Jocy.

Jack went back to his office, and I went looking for my clipboard. My *magic* clipboard. It helps me think clearly and to discover what I really want to know about anything I had going on.

My clipboard was where I left it, in my loft, on my blue leather chair. I kicked off my boots, picked up my pen, and pulled my feet up on the blue ottoman.

The words poured from my heart onto the page.

'I've met the girl I want to be with. There seems to be an underlying story going on with her. I will be led to the correct way to her heart, while being buffered and protected along the way.'

That was enough. I spent the rest of the day answering correspondence from readers, and making notes for my next book. Then ready for bed, I set my cell phone to wake me at five a.m.

ELEVEN

My loft was five minutes walking distance from Jocy's gallery. One of the perks of being a financially successful writer is having more than one place to call home. I love my Manhattan loft, and it keeps me in the middle of all things connected with the book world. And now it connects me to Jocy.

A clear, warm spring morning with Starbucks in my hand, and off to have a great morning especially one with Jocy in it.

Just as I rounded the corner near her gallery, she's coming out the door, appearing to be looking for someone. Catching my eye, I realize it's me she's looking for. She's dressed casual in jeans, a crisp white blouse and a blue denim blazer. We could be twins. I was in my Levi's, boots, denim shirt and suede jacket. My face lit up as we got closer.

She moved toward me. Gently grabbing my arm she said, "How about Starbucks?" Those were words of love as far I was concerned. Starbucks plus Jocy. Perfection in a moment.

Not wasting any time, her arm in mine, she told me that her gallery had cameras and microphones. We would have a few private moments on the way to coffee and back. There was something of extreme importance she needed for me to know, and I needed to know it now.

First she told me I looked like Brad Pitt, the Brad Pitt from 'Meet Joe Black'. She liked me, I could tell. She knew I liked her. Words of affection would go unspoken for now, as something else was pressing on her mind.

Jocy began, "I got hooked up with the wrong people. Dangerous people. They control the world's purse strings. Unknown to me, the horses that I was bringing from overseas were used to smuggle stolen artwork. By the time I figured out what was going on, it was too late. I was going to be framed for stealing this artwork, if I didn't 'play along'. People that I cared about would be hurt. I had no choice."

I said nothing, sensing that she had more to say.

"You Hank, you have become an unwanted distraction for this group. The things you write about, the things you teach others are a threat to the string around the purse. The good news is, they want me to pursue a relationship with you, so that they can keep you close. This could be fun, except it involves me lying to you about many—"

I stopped her mid-sentence. "Why am I a distraction, other than the type of writing I do?"

"The consortium that you and Jack are developing will involve many of the same money-people who are unknowingly part of the stolen artwork cartel. They think that if you become too involved, your curiosity would blow open their neat and tidy financial outlet, which involves not only millions but billions of dollars. They want me to keep you close to me, which keeps you close to them."

Jocy went on to explain how they smuggled the valuable artwork into the country.

"You've seen the film, 'The Thomas Crown Affair' right?"

"Yes, it's actually my favorite of all time. Why?"

"In the beginning of the film, they show in the basement of the art museum a large crate with a giant Trojan horse inside, which is where the thieves were hiding."

"Yes, go on."

"There are two ways to ship horses from overseas to the US. One is by air and the other is by ship or sea freight. There are companies with expertise in both methods, and the animals are always well cared for."

"Go on."

She said, "For the purposes of my so-called 'associates' they always choose sea freight, as it is safe and stress-free horse transport. It's also the most cost effective. Professional traveling grooms and customized accommodations are provided and sea freight allows for faster recovery times for the horses. Also, it is easier to monitor the shipment and the employees involved in shipping.

"I have to say that in spite of their overall intentions and plans, they were respectful of my care of the horses and followed any suggestions that I offered. On the other hand, they also had their own people in place and on their payroll when it came to the grooms provided, as well as people on the payroll at the customs and quarantine desks and final veterinarian sign-offs.

"Within each bay provided for each horse was a hidden panel. Before and after each loading and unloading of the horses, along with the authorized safety authorities, who were also on their payroll, these panels were lifted from the ship. Looking as innocent crates with proper (fraudulent) papers, they slid onto large trucks and onto the final destination."

I said, "Well, that explains a lot. But Jocy, it seems you know the intricate details of how they implement the shipment of artwork. Aren't you concerned that you know too much?"

"Oh, I know way too much," she agreed. "But they've grown to trust me to some extent. For the moment they need me to keep their little or not-so-little enterprise moving along smoothly. They know how many of the wealthy in the art and equine worlds depend on my services." She looked at me squarely. "But I want out."

"...What I am gathering from what you're telling me, Jocy, is that you want me to play along. Being with you is the easy part. I want to find out where this thing between us is going. I mean, I haven't met anyone that has turned my head and flipped my heart the way you have done. But what do you see as the end game here, Jocy? If at some level we are 'pretending' to be attracted to each other, what does that mean for *us*."

Her words came out fast. "Hank, the end game is I want out. I don't know how to get out. Meeting you was not an accident. It was an answered prayer. I know it was. I'm so sure that you can help me that I'm not feeling a bit guilty about asking for your help. I know you are here to help me."

"Jocy, yes, of course we can figure this out as we go along. Make it up as we go. But Jocy, what do we do about Shawn? He seems to keep a pretty watchful eye over you."

"That's exactly it. He's around to watch me. But since you are added to the plan, he will lessen the reigns so that you and I develop a relationship."

"Where do they think you are now, at this early hour? Won't they be suspicious?"

"No, their plan for you and me began yesterday. I was to purposely have you meet me early, so that you would 'think' something was up."

"Well that worked out perfectly."

"Yes, what they don't know is that I have a plan within a plan."

"Ok, Jocy. How do we begin?"

"Hank, we begin by seeing one another frequently. We enjoy one another. We have fun."

"…Okay… …I can do that." (Place Huge Blonde-Boy Handsome Smile, here.)

TWELVE

After leaving Jocy, I headed back to my loft. Like the writer, Graham Greene, I owned a private and secure loft, keeping my address and phone number secret from everyone except my best friend and publisher, Jack Wade, and one other confidant, Sam Jamison.

The New York City Streets were full of their usual morning bustle and energy. My loft was near both Wall Street and Central Park. A Starbucks was around the corner, my next stop. They know me there. As soon as I hit the counter, I hear, "Large Café Mocha for Hank!"

Walking out, coffee in hand, I suddenly became aware that I am being watched. Pretending not to notice I called Jack. We needed an idea and I had one. I needed to run it by Jack and then Jocy.

"Jack, I have an idea for the consortium. Do you have time to meet?"

"Sure. How 'bout lunch at The Wall Street Café. I've got a meeting there at ten a.m.," he said.

"Great, see you at noon."

It was still early morning. Deciding to see what I could find out about Jocy and the people she was involved with, I knew my next move. I needed to talk to my friend Sam.

Sam is discreet. He has helped me remain private in my world of publishing fame. I would have to contact him from my loft, as all of my communications are buffered and protected from unwanted intrusion. He had designed the setup, and was connected in the same way.

Sam and I had ties to a hidden, private world. There are three worlds: the underworld, the perceived world (where mass humanity operates from, which contains man made laws) and a completely sealed world. It was from this hermetically sealed world that I was able to become famous yet maintain my privacy.

The only way into this hidden world was through a 'Hierogram', a sacred coded message. Only Jack, Sam and I had this code.

Knowing that my phone was probably bugged, this was one occasion where a burner phone would come in handy for my call to Sam. But there wouldn't be time to get a burner before my meeting with Jack. Before I could consider what I wanted to do next, my phone rings. It's Jocy. How did she get my number? I hadn't given it to her yet.

Wanting to trust her, but not convinced that I understood the situation, I decided to just follow along to see what would show itself. I could tell from her voice that this was a follow-up call about us spending time together. Coming so soon probably wasn't her idea.

I mentioned that Jack and I were getting together to discuss my idea for Consortium, and I invited her to meet us. She would be there. The three of us would meet soon enough, but I really wanted to spend more time getting to know her. Meeting me at eleven a.m. at the Café, an hour earlier than the meeting with Jack, would give us a little time. Getting her alone would help me find out more. I wanted to see if my first instincts were correct: maybe she could be The One.

THIRTEEN

The café was near an entrance to Central Park. I specifically chose the park for our get-to-know-each-other stroll because I knew of three electronic dead spots. Our conversations would not be overheard or picked up by anyone. These dead zones are only known to Jack, Sam and me. Sam is the one who designed the electronic dead zones.

There was no dead zone between Jocy and me. The second our eyes locked, as we came toward the café from different directions, the air between us felt charged with electricity. How could the people rushing along the sidewalk not feel the heat?

We walked and talked for about ten minutes, getting to know one another. It was her wit, her beauty, her intelligence that drew me in. However, I still couldn't help but wonder how someone so savvy allowed herself to become a pawn in an unsafe and unsavory operation. I was eager to find out.

What I was about to hear from those soft, plum-colored lips made all thought stop.

Gently, my hand in the small of her back, I guided us toward the dead zone where we sat side by side on a bench. I felt the electricity. I wanted to kiss her, but didn't. Time was of the essence. I assured her that our conversation could not be overheard or recorded. No one would hear any of it. I didn't want to tell her about Sam just yet, but I knew he was watching out for us.

Jocy broke the silence. "My brother was a CIA operative. He got too close to the wrong side of the money. I was sent a video of him captive and being tortured, and then shot. They killed him. Without skipping a beat, they threatened the same to anyone I loved or cared about. They knew them all, all relatives, all friends, lovers and business acquaintances."

With her eyes tearing, she continued: "I didn't have time to process what I had just been shown. I was in a state of both shock and fright. At first I didn't know what they wanted from me. Very quickly the picture became clear. A messenger showed up at my condo door. This wasn't just any messenger. I knew I must see him when a picture of my brother was shoved up at the peephole in the door."

My hands were closed over hers. I didn't dare say a word to interrupt her story.

She continued. "Slowly backing away, not saying a word, I let him in. He finally offered an introduction of sorts."

"He said, 'I'm not here to harm you Ms. Jocy, I'm simply a messenger. But I suggest you listen and cooperate. May I sit down?' He took a seat without waiting for me to say anything. He said, 'You and I are in similar spots, rough ones. I am being asked to do things against my will, and against the law, just as you will be. We have no alternative. I'm sure they threatened to harm all that is precious to you.'"

"Yes they have," Jocy went on with the horrific story. "What do they want from me?"

"The man said, 'You are to be a front of sorts, a delivery system for stolen art and antiques, much of which is procured by them from overseas. You do not, I repeat, do not have a choice.

These are very powerful people connected to all forms of financial resources. They are the ones who control the purse strings of the money bags all over the world.'"

"He told me to expect further instructions, and then he got up and left. He didn't tell me how I would be given these instructions."

Jocy took a long breath. "I couldn't imagine my way out of this until you showed up, Hank. Maybe you're my way out. They know you are extremely wealthy, but they don't know how you have accumulated your wealth, or where you keep it. They want me to find out, and they are counting on my relationship with you taking on more intimate dynamics."

As she is telling me this profound story, my mind is losing focus. I'm between anger and lust. I need to keep my head on straight and my pants zipped, if I'm to be any good to any of us.

"Hank, you know I would be using you, trying to convince them that I was giving them what they wanted."

"Yes, Jocy. I understand, but what about you? The part of you that is between using me for your freedom while giving them what they want?"

She said nothing.

"How did they come to find out about my well-guarded wealth?"

"As you know, it's difficult to keep anything hidden these days, and of course I'm not supposed to tell you this, but..."

"But what?"

"It was when you began inquiring about exclusive property near Necker Island. You know, the one owned by Richard Branson."

"Yes, of course, go on. Those inquiries were to be kept confidential."

"Yes, well, the broker you were using was a confidant of another broker who was not as trustworthy as yours. A better way to put this, they had something as leverage to use against the other broker. In exchange for information as to who was looking to buy, they would release him of his 'debt'. That's how they came to know of you and your interest in the property."

"Well, certainly I'm not the only person looking at investments in that area of the world. Why me?"

"Hank, they are aware of your writing success, but they became curious as to just how much you acquired that seemed to be outside the boundaries of what successful writers are likely to earn in a short period of time. That was the red flag. That was what caught their attention, your name showing up as an interested party near Necker Island, and more importantly that you were willing to pay cash."

"Ok, I see. But what about you, Jocy? The part of you that is between using me for your freedom, while giving them what they want?"

Jocy lowered her head. "I've been in limbo for so long, I don't know if I can connect to an answer. I've been their puppet for so long, I can't think my way out of this." She looked up, looking directly into my eyes. "And Hank, I know you are wondering if you can trust me. Yet here you are."

"Yes, Jocy. And this, you and me, and whatever shakes out … this is a risk I'm willing to take."

I took her hand again as we stood by the bench. Knowing we were leaving the dead zone, I whispered, "Let's see where this takes us." I was implying for the sake of possible romance, but in both our minds we knew more was at stake than that. If the romance were true, it would simply make it all sweeter and 'the juice worth the squeeze'.

FOURTEEN

Then it was time for us to meet Jack. We walked swiftly, hand in hand. It was as if we were on automatic, already in sync with one another.

It had been a long time since I had this feeling of warmth and affection towards someone. As I was lost in thought, Jocy's phone chimes. She let go of my hand and stepped away. We were in front of the Café and I could see Jack through the window, waving us over.

Jocy looks over at me, and puts her phone back in her pocket. "That was Shawn, Hank. I have to take a rain check on lunch. Please extend my apology to Jack." Just then a black Mercedes limo pulls over the curb, apparently for her. In a slight whisper, as she kisses me on the cheek, she says, "It begins."

As I stood there in a daze, Jack tapped on the restaurant window, signaling for me to come in.

"Did you see that, Jack?" I said as I took a seat at his table.

"Jocy leaving? Yes. I take it her plans changed at the last minute?" He leaned toward me and said in a hushed voice, "Hank, I know you like the girl. As I said, everyone does. Be careful. Oh and Hank, Sam is on it."

"On What?"

"On The limo and the boyfriend."

"Ok, great. Thanks for reminding me. I should have remembered. My mind, well, my thoughts…"

"Hank, I know. It's Jocy. I know.

"Yes."

"Can you focus on why we are here, or do I have to put up with this lovesick face all through lunch?"

"Of course, sorry, I'm present and here. In fact I have an idea and a name for the consortium.

"I'm listening."

"Bogarts- A Bookstore Channel for Independent Writers and Artists."

"Hank, I like it! But Hank you do know that somehow Jocy and her associates may become involved in this as well, simply due to the nature of the art world and the people in it. It could be dangerous for all of us, if you get more involved with her."

It was at this point that I needed to remind Jack of what we were really about. I needed to remind myself as well, before being blindsided by interest in Jocy.

FIFTEEN

My friendship with Jack began in the third grade. I had a vivid experience with a 'mean person'. It was my third grade teacher, Mrs McAdams. She was reprimanding me for something by pulling on my ears. It hurt to say the least, on top of being humiliated in class. I had no power; she was the teacher. I was going to have to just take it, or it might have been worse.

Jack had lived next door and was in that same class with me. He waited until recess that day and then pulled me to aside. Little did I know at the time, this was to set the direction of our lives. Grabbing my shoulders, looking me square in the face he said, "Hank, when we get big, we're gonna be in charge. People won't be mean to us anymore!"

Jack's youthful wisdom would set the course of our lives past our rooming together at UVA, and beyond. I watched him build his business and marry the girl of his dreams. His connections would be envied by presidents, heads of state, as well as by the rich and famous.

And he was my best friend to the core.

Although he was my mentor of sorts, through the osmosis of our friendship, my own direction began to show itself: ideas, thoughts, and unique approaches to a better world. I knew whatever was to take place, it would have to start with me.

SIXTEEN

I studied anything and everything related to the esoteric from the East to the West and back again. Then, one day it happened.

One day while on the phone with someone asking my advice on a particular challenge they were having, the conversation changed. Something or someone else was on the other end. As much as I had studied, I never knew of an instance where I was consciously aware of being contacted from some other plane or realm. This voice was very clear and succinct. Non-threatening, matter of fact, it was telling me to go to the computer for a two-way communication. This was through an instant messaging application. I did as I was told, never questioning what was happening.

The words coming through on the other end were clear and concise. "You, Hank Ramsan, you will bring to the world the ease and promise of the Alladin's Lamp fable. It will be as easy as your Jeannie in the TV show, *I Dream of Jeannie*. You will label this new information, which is not new, but will be new in understanding, *GeniSourceOlogy*. You will bring the Promise of all ancient texts to the contemporary world. That is all for now."

I sat there, dumbfounded, numb for a moment and then inspiration and excitement flooded my mind and body. It was with that phone call and cyber message that my path to *Privately Famous* began.

Famous, to the extent that my writing would become internationally known with the accompanying wealth and success. *Privately,* as I would remain private, buffered and protected in my life and livelihood while implementing *GeniSourceOlogy* for myself and then for others.

Unknown to me back then, I would soon find out what this had to do with Jocy and our relationship.

SEVENTEEN

The perfect opportunity showed for Jocy and me to spend time together. Jack called reminding me to be on a panel at a writers' conference in Virginia. I wasted no time inviting Jocy. She said yes, and we agreed to meet for dinner to discuss plans.

Charlottesville VA was my first home, and I love it there. Its connection to both writing and privacy is important to me. Many famous writers and celebrities live there. We don't travel in the same circles, as most writers lead a life of isolation and solitude.

As I waited for Jocy in the lobby of the Four Seasons, I noticed a familiar face near the elevator. *Shawn.* Jocy's so-called boyfriend.

Just as I glanced his way, "Hank?" came from a soft voice behind me.

"Hello Jocy, you look wonderful!"

"Thank you Hank. I've been looking forward to this evening."

"Jocy, anything I should know about Shawn creeping around?"

"He's keeping an eye on me, on us."

"Ok, well let's head to the dining room and plan our Charlottesville trip." I turned to her wanting to know, "Shawn is aware of my inviting you to Charlottesville, right?"

"Oh, yes. "*They* see it as an opportunity to find out more about you, more about your wealth connections. By the way, where will we be staying?"

"I have a home on five acres with a heliopad. We'll fly down in Wade Publishing's Private Jet and then helicopter on to my home. If you prefer to stay in a hotel, I can put you up in the Omni." I added, "Jocy, I hope you know I'll be a gentleman, as well as watch out for you."

"Hank, no concerns on my end. I know you have my best interest at heart. I look forward to it."

Jocy began asking about the art world and various homes around Albemarle County. She knew The Kluges were once there and Donald Trump and his sons had purchased the property, including the Kluge Estate.

I assured her that I could put her in touch with the elite of the area, including art enthusiasts.

Our dinner conversation remained light and casual, until she finally broached the subject of my financial resources.

"Hank, you know they want me to find out about your secrets, your money."

"Yes, I know. Don't they also know that I understand your real intent? I mean, why play this game?"

"It's just their way of pretending to get what they want by being polite. If the 'polite way' according to how they define it, doesn't work, then they would resort to more impolite means."

"Well, Jocy, I don't have any secrets. My financials are documented, except for that which is hidden. And that which is hidden is less about secrets and more about an elite force that I have access to, and that's all I'll say for now."

We both felt the moment approaching a tenseness. She was being pushed to get information from me that I was unwilling to disclose. This made it uncomfortable for both of us, since there also was an underlying attraction that we both wanted to 'get to'. I knew her next question would be about 'The Elite Force', and that was privy only to Jack, Sam and myself.

My hopes for a romantic dinner were fading fast. This had turned into a business meeting, and an uncomfortable one at that. I still wasn't completely sure if I could trust Jocy, or where her true intentions would lead. Finding out would be both interesting and challenging.

While in the midst of conversation, the waiter appeared with the check.

"Thank you, but we've not ordered dessert yet," I said.

"Yes, Sir, Mr. Ramsan, I was asked to give you a message with the check."

I opened the pad containing the check. There was a message all right. "Hank, beware of your female companion." It was signed, A Benefactor.

I showed it to Jocy.

She sighed, wearily. "Hank, I'm not surprised you're being warned about me. I've had to mislead and manipulate others, and if I wouldn't, eventually, they or I would suffer the consequences."

While pretending to sign the check, I scribbled a note showing it to her. "Are you wearing a wire?"

Her eyes answered, 'yes'.

I knew I needed to get us both somewhere where we could speak freely. But that moment would have to wait.

Things were moving too slowly with me and Jocy. This wasn't like the usual courtship. This was 'three's a crowd.' The third party was unknown to me at the moment. Maybe it was a dangerous party. If so, was she worth the risk I might have to take?

Yes. Yes it is.

EIGHTEEN

While working on my next book, I could involve Jocy in some way. This was what I was thinking.

This could give us some common ground to help me get to know her better. Her task of trying to find out more about my finances and connections would be part of the deal. The subject of my new book, while entertaining, is also filled with 'Gems of Antiquity'. Gems of Antiquity would mean one thing to some and something entirely different to others. This would also help me uncover the nefarious group controlling Jocy, while finding out what they were up to.

Since our relationship was moving slower than I like, unlike New York, which never sleeps nor stands still; publishing houses had gotten wind of my new book. They were trying to get me to sell out, or switch from Wade Worldwide. That wasn't going to happen. Jack already has my book, and any book or idea I will ever have. He always would, just as Sam has my back. They have been the ones I have trusted with everything near and dear all along. It was time for us to meet to set an agenda.

No one could know about the special meeting between the three of us.

The three of us are seldom seen in public together. There is a unique reason for this. From my loft, I slid the hidden panel to a gateway. Only Jack, Sam and I know of this gateway. Pressing a button, which actually looks like a button you would see on a coat or blazer, which makes it inconspicuous, a signal is sent to both Jack and Sam to meet at three p.m. It's always an unspoken understanding that we meet at three p.m.

We all reach the meeting by different routes. Jack and I arrive first, Sam moments later.

This place we meet is unlike any conference or meeting room. It's more like an Ivy League library, rich in texture and depth. Other rich and famous people have access to this hall. Not just any rich and famous, however. But for now, it's just us three.

Jack takes the lead. "Hank, it's time for your next book. Do you have a title, a theme?"

"Yes, as a matter of fact, I do. 'Gems of Antiquity'."

Jack immediately caught the double meaning.

Sam was a bit in the dark, and asked the question: "Will this book discuss how you achieved your wealth? That's fine up to this point. Jack and I have been the only ones to know. Are you thinking of disclosing the information in this new book?"

"Yes, Sam, but only those of a higher consciousness will be able to decipher the 'how'. To others it will have a message similar to a fairy tale. And as you know, most fairy tales are hidden truths." I looked at them closely. "What I want to know gentlemen is what role Jocy will play in this? It's no accident that she's in the picture."

"Hank, let's just begin as we would any book project, and we'll see what shows up," Jack offered in his usual business sense.

All of us agreed.

NINTEEN

The common denominator first showed up for the three of us in childhood. We all lived on the same street. Being boys filled with curiosity and a spirit for adventure, one day we stumbled upon a cave at the edge of our small town.

We grew up in a time when children could roam freely. Parents didn't worry if we were gone for hours. Being gone for hours lead us on an adventure of a lifetime. This would play itself out as we grew into young university students, and then into our livelihoods.

Jack and I were always on the fringe of the writing and publishing world. Sam, on the other hand was led in a different direction, one that would benefit us all as the years showed themselves.

The cave was the beginning of it all.

As it happened, it was around three p.m. one hot, sunny afternoon. We had ridden our bikes to the end of the county line, not far from the main street of the town. The county line stopped abruptly at the base of a mountain. We all hit the brakes at the end of a dirt gravel road. Ashy dust went flying. When the dust finally settled, Sam noticed a sign. "Look guys!"

The sign was in the shape of a triangle, wooden and dusty, with cut letters carved into the wood. Sam climbed down off his bike first to get a closer look. Jack and I stayed straddling ours.

The sign wasn't stuck in the ground but it was heavy enough that wind or rain wouldn't likely move it from its place.

"Sam, what does the sign say?" Jack wanted to know as he dismounts his bike with me following close behind. Our view was obstructed by some large boulders.

Sam called over his shoulder, "You guys gotta see this!"

There was no fear in Sam's voice, mostly excitement, as he motioned for us to move around the boulders and come closer.

The three of us stood mesmerized as we silently read the words on the sign: Au4U HJS.

We knew from our science class and the politics at the time that Au was the symbol for Gold. We felt a surge of excitement and wonder as Sam read other initials on the sign, "*H J S.*"

I'm not sure how long we stood there looking at the strange sign before Jack said, "Hey guys, it's getting late. We should head home. We don't want anyone to come looking for us."

Sam and I agreed. I suggested we all meet at the baseball diamond at ten the following morning with packed lunches. We'd use my mom as the parent in charge. The other parents would be comfortable with that, and we could spend all day discovering whatever we were to discover at the base of the mountain.

TWENTY

At ten a.m. sharp the next morning, we all showed up with knapsacks full of chips and cookies. Jack was in charge of the canteens of water. He carried three. We were ready, bikes charged, sunny morning; we headed back to the county line.

The sign was where we left it. Sam was careful to cover it with dirt and brush, keeping it hidden from view.

"This Way!" Sam pointed to the left. There seemed to be a path, barely recognizable. We trusted Sam's intuition and followed. Jack, then me.

The path wasn't worn-looking, as if it had been traveled. It just seemed to show the way for us somehow. We started on a downward dissent, coasting while keeping our brakes on, ready to stop on a moment's notice.

Sam abruptly stopped. Jack almost slid into him. And there we were at the bottom of this path, with green grass mounds closing the path on both sides. In front of us, nothing but more Ivy covered rocks and large boulders. Just as we were wondering if this was a dead end, and if we had chosen the wrong path, roses started blooming on the mound in front of us. We were boys and we knew nothing about flowers, but we knew this was not normal. We stood still just watching them bloom, and looking at each other with wonder. Hundreds of blooms, and then they started to shape a doorway.

The rose petals started to drop to the ground. A new path and the door were made clear. Its form was a perfect rounded doorway, first filled with rose petals, then dropping to show the opening.

It was clear. We were to walk through the rose petal doorway.

Sam, by this time, had dropped his bike. Jack and I were still holding onto ours. Sam looked back at us as if to say, "It's ok. Let go of your bikes."

We slowly walked in.

There was an energy that felt warm, not cool as you might feel in most areas around caves and caverns. The further we went, the more the pathway seemed to be lit by some type of natural light shining down through the cavern. It was like it was meant just for us. It *was* just for us.

We walked slowly, which felt like forever, but was only about fifteen minutes. Single file: Sam, Jack, then me. We came to an open space where there were natural rock formations in the shape of three benches. These benches seemed to be inviting us to sit. We each chose one and sat quietly, waiting for who knows what.

We weren't really afraid. I'm not sure why. But we weren't. We sat there looking at one another.

Then, somehow, we heard a voice in our heads. We all heard it. "For your lifetime you will be brothers—you will protect each other for what is to become."

Then we heard the voice say, "Hank, go to the wall on your right. Place your right hand on the wall three feet above the ground."

Since I was only twelve, three feet was right about my heart area. When I pressed my hand against the wall, I felt a light pressure as something lay against my palm. I didn't feel any fear, only wonder. Slowly, I looked down at my hand, which now held a golden crystal. It fit snuggly into my palm, being about the size of a silver dollar. It appeared to be in the shape of a pineapple.

I turned around and showed it to Jack and Sam. They huddled over to me to get a closer look.

Then we heard, "Hank Ramsan, the Knowledge of The Ancients is stored in this gold crystal. It will speak to you intuitively. Keep it with you always. If you lose it, or it is taken, it will always find its way back to you."

The voice continued: "If you lose it, all you need to do is envision holding it in your palm, just as you are doing right now. It will guide you to its location. You are the only one it will speak to."

The voice answered the question that we were all thinking: "What role did Jack and Sam have to play in *this?*"

The Answer came: "Hank, you will write the books. Jack, you will publish them. Sam, you will protect them both from harm. You will create extraordinary resources to help them both."

I could not help but feel skeptical. "Me? Write books?" This had to be a mistake.

I heard the voice again: "A time will come when readers will be ready to understand the truths you will teach about the ancients. When this time comes, you will be prepared to write.

You need not understand everything right now. Keep the crystal close. Keep noticing what you notice."

And so ... that was the beginning of our mission together: *To bring happiness, joy, abundance and prosperity to humanity based on the knowledge first given by at least two ancient civilizations. All of which was easier than anyone had spoken of since.*

TWENTY ONE

As the years went by, the three of us remained close, even though our livelihoods would have us travel in different circles. My home base was in Virginia, while often visiting New York, since Jack was there publishing my writing.

Sam, on the other hand, often went underground to do whatever he did. Much of his life was secretive, due to working with various clandestine associations. Jack and I respected his position and never pushed for information. But now, something was up. None of us knew what exactly, but it had something to do with Jocy and her involvement with mysterious individuals unknown to us.

Our three p.m. meeting came to a close. We had an agenda. Jocy would travel to Charlottesville as we'd planned, and I'd begin writing my next book. Jack would begin things on the promotion end. Readers were anxious for my next title. Sam would keep a watchful eye on Jocy and find out more about the group that seemed to have some control over her, and which she wanted so badly to escape.

TWENTY TWO

When I called Jocy to make final plans for our trip to Virginia, I kept it cryptic. I could tell she wasn't free to talk, so I kept it short. "Jocy, you still ok to meet me at ten tomorrow morning?"

"Yes Hank. I'll be ready. See you then."

That was it. No warmth, just matter of fact. But I would get more from her tomorrow.

For now I needed to plan my talk for the writers' panel. I knew the questions to expect: "How did I achieve my success? What habits did I form? Do I have any shortcuts to writing success?" As always, I held the pineapple-shaped golden crystal in my right hand while a thought about these things. *What should I say? How much should I say?*

My answers would be similar to any successful writer, all expect for one thing. And for that I'd have to read the audience to see just how much they would be ready to hear.

Writing success was my way of opening people up to an easier more enjoyable way to move through life. Writing was the tool I was using, but Higher Law was the method. Recognizing the importance of good storytelling to produce an impact, it was always my intention to be entertaining while writing between the lines. Some would intuitively 'hear and see'. For others, possibly a crack in their consciousness would allow the light in.

But first, with a few free days, it was on to the West Coast for a little fun work, and companionship.

Notes on 3x5 cards ready-packed for three days, cell phone alarm set for five a.m. Early rising was part of my success and how I spent those early hours. I would especially need this time for whatever Jocy was bringing to the table.

TWENTY THREE

Promptly at ten a.m. the Wade limo stopped in front of Jocy's studio. She was watching from the window, like she was anxious to get going ... at least that's what I wanted to believe. She waved and greeted me at the door, overnight bag in hand.

"Mornin', Jocy. You look great!"

She smiled. She was wearing jeans, short dingos, a crisp white button down blouse with soft ruffles at the top, a waist length brown suede jacket that complimented her look. She always looked 'together and fresh.' My hand took hers, helping her into the limo. I felt a warm surge.

Sam was our driver, but I pretended he was simply a Wade employee, so as not to draw attention to him.

Sitting next to her in the car, but not too close, I reached into my pocket and pulled out a green 3x5 card. I jotted down words, showing it to Jocy. "Wire?"

She read the card and smiled that beautiful smile. She said, nonchalantly, "Nope. They assumed we might get close and you finding a wire as you unbuttoned my blouse would not be a good thing."

We both roared in laughter, releasing some of the tension.

"No Hank," she continued, "No wire, but you know they are tracking my phone."

"Yes, I figured that much. If we pretended to lose it, they would know something was up. We don't need to ruffle their feathers just yet."

"Yes. True, plus Hank they expect me to answer when they call, so having my phone close is part of the arrangement."

"Jocy, do they have any inkling that I know there's more to this, whatever *this* is? I mean more than you've told me about your situation?"

"No, Hank. They know me only as very loyal. They are not suspicious, but I'll have to give them something from our time together."

Sam interrupted the moment. "Mr. Ramsan, we're at the Wall St. Heliport. I'll pull up so you and Ms. Jocy can be on your way."

Closing the door, my eyes met Sam's. As always his were communicating, "Don't worry. I've got your back."

TWENTY FOUR

We ran to the helicopter, with the blades swirling above our heads. We hastily entered, seated and buckled up.

The Wade Helicopter wasn't just any helicopter. It was the top-of-the-line elite. It was a $13-million, Sikorski S-76-c. Its range was more than enough to get us to Charlottesville. What Jocy didn't know, we'd be making a detour, a stop along the way to Virginia. I had a surprise in mind for her. An event of Famous Living Artists.

Taking advantage of the pleasure and spontaneity that usually comes with a new relationship, at least mine, it was important that Jocy feel safe in whatever I was planning. Keeping the surprise intact, and her *overseers* unaware, would be to my advantage.

"Jocy, I have a surprise for you. We have a stop to make before landing in Charlottesville. For this, we need to change vehicles."

"Uh, Hank, is that a landing strip down there in the middle of nowhere?"

"Sure is, another perk of being a Wade Writer: we're taking Jack's jet to the West Coast. This trip is for business and pleasure, so Jack can deduct it. I've got two impromptu book signings. One is at the Bank of Books in Malibu, and the gorgeous Barnes & Nobel in Calabasis. From there, I thought we'd visit the J. Paul Getty Center in L.A. Your eyes can take in Van Gogh, Monet and Rembrandts's self-portrait, (Laughing)."

The helicopter touched down and Jocy's eyes met mine with a warm approving smile for our detour. We were still in cell phone range, but that would soon change as the altitude and coverage would be limited. I could have about ninety minutes of private conversation with Jocy.

She was concerned. Just as we were about to board the plane, she said, "Hank, I need to touch base with them. If I go out of range for too long, they'll become suspicious. I need to let them know our plans and that I may be out of range for a bit, understand?"

"Sure, of course." Then, "To make it less conspicuous, I'll escort you to the plane and then excuse myself for the restroom and snacks. Will that give you enough time for your conversation?"

"Yes, Hank. Thanks. That'll work."

So far, so good. I'm still feeling pretty good about my plans for our day. Jocy will be anxious-free after she reports in and we'll get to relax in flight. Who knows what may come?

TWENTY FIVE

Jocy returned to her seat, smiling.

"Do I get to know what the smiles are about?"

"Of course. They've given me free reign on this trip. They did ask who you thought I was calling so soon into our trip."

"And you said?"

"I told them that I told you, I needed to touch base with a client about a meeting. They were satisfied. So Hank, I feel the weight off of me. Now I can enjoy our trip."

The plane ride was filled with peace, calm and laughter. I got to know more about Jocy, and what makes her happy. She talked about her love for horses, and shared several amusing memories. When she talked about art, I saw that we felt the same way about finding innovative ways for unknown artists and writers to share their work. I'd become smitten, and now my feelings were taking a new turn. One that I hoped she would welcome.

Wondering, asking aloud about her level of happiness, under the circumstances she was in … was there any relief?

Her answer was revealing. "I've made many great friends, celebrities, funny people, interesting and smart people. They are my joy, these relationships. The only downside of some of these relationships is that I have to manipulate some of them."

"Can you give me a *for instance?*"

"There is an older couple—old money, family money. They loved and trusted me like a daughter. They trusted me to guide some of their investments in the art world. I suggested some paintings that I knew were forgeries. But they would never be the wiser." After a long pause she continued. "The real painting was diverted to my associates, and the forgeries were shipped to my friends. To this day they don't know about the switch."

'What happens, Jocy, should they decide to sell them. Won't they be found out?"

"No. Most likely they would ask me to handle the sale, and by that time any profit from the sale would be maximized, or otherwise justified. But Hank, you're going to find a way to get me out of all of this, right?"

"I'll do my best. In the meantime, we have three wonderful days in California."

It was impossible to think about anything beyond those three days with Jocy.

TWENTY SIX

The combination was perfect. A little wine and freedom from that other world.

As Jocy got up to reach for the overhead compartment, there was a slight turbulence bumping her onto my lap.

It was an uneasy moment for both of us. I'd like to think it was sexual tension. But then she took my face in her hands, gently placing her lips on mine.

I could have died a happy man right then. The joy and other feelings that ran through my body were unlike any I had felt before, for anyone.

She slowly pulled her face away from mine—her eyes smiling. Raising herself up to her feet, as if to brush herself off, she said, "Ok, then!"

Amazement mode took on the symptom of silence in my own head. Glancing affectionately at me, she too seemed affected by the moment. We were both quiet as she dosed off in a relaxed, slightly intoxicated state.

A nap seemed like a good idea, as we would be adding three hours to our day, due to time zone differences.

Into a deep sleep, I was awakened by the voice of the pilot. "Mr. Ramsan, time to buckle up."

We were circling the landing strip. Jocy was awake and adjusting her makeup. We still hadn't spoken since the kiss.

So far, wine-kisses and naps. Not a bad start to a new adventure. ...That kiss would have to hold me for a while.

TWENTY SEVEN

Jack arranged for his office in Malibu to meet us with a car. Such are the benefits of success.

I hadn't always been this successful, but when I hit my stride it just kept growing. The growth, the *how* was of Ancient Knowledge. I studied it, understood it and applied it. Whether Jocy would be privy to any of this remained to be seen.

The driver knew the area well. We spent a few hours at The Getty drinking up the richness of the old Masters until it was time to head to the first book signing.

The day was filled with fun and relaxation. The kiss still wasn't mentioned. It's like it would spoil the memory if we talked about it, so we didn't.

Our day ended with dinner at an outdoor café. The California weather makes us easterners yearn to stay outdoors.

Wade Publishing was putting us up in its condo. Once we arrived there, we decided that Jocy would take the upstairs bedroom and I the downstairs.

We said our goodnights, both being polite. But a few moments later, she came down the stairs, as if she forgot something. She wore a light T-shirt, which I noticed right away as I turned from closing the condo door. She was on the landing and I was a breath away from her. We looked at one another. I didn't, couldn't move. She took me by the hand, led me up the stairs. My life will never be the same.

I became putty in her hands, but I wasn't sure this was a completely good thing yet.

The next morning I was startled awake by a phone ringing. It was Jocy's. With one eye open, I could see it was 7 a.m.

She seemed a bit shaken as she hung up.

"What?"

"That was Shawn—he's here."

"What do you mean, here?"

"He's in Malibu."

"What happened to him loosening the grip on you?"

"Seems he's the jealous type."

"What does he want?"

"He wants me to meet him."

As she puts on her robe, I see the outline of her slender, beautiful body. She turns to me and smiles, but still no conversation about what happened.

"Hank, I'm gonna get a shower. I'll start the coffee first, and then I'll have to go."

"Jocy? Will you be ok?"

"Yes, I'm too valuable to them for him to hurt me."

"Sure?"

"Sure. I'll meet him while you're in Calabasas at the BN book signing. I'll call him now so it's set and we can enjoy a little bit of our morning."

Jocy left the bedroom to call him. I didn't try to listen. I decided to trust her.

But I didn't like this.

TWENTY EIGHT

A Few Words From Me, Jocy...

While Hank's in the shower, I'll give you some background from my side of the story.

Before I got myself in this jam, I was already successful in my own business. I made it on my own with lots of friends along the way, which made me attractive to unsavory types.

This same success in the high fashion of art and equestrian venues made me a target for the people I hope Hank can free me from.

Although I have met many nice and equally successful single (and married) men, I've never felt free to let myself go with any of them, until now, until Hank.

Both Hank and I know I'm in a precarious position, having to use him, while also wanting to be with him. But I'm trusting in the overall good, trusting that the unknown goodness will prevail. I just hope this goodness appears before anyone else, especially those I love and care for, can be hurt or worse.

Ok. Hank's out of the shower now, so I must go back to my world, the rest is up to Hank Ramsan.

TWENTY NINE

"Jocy, while I was in the shower, it occurred to me how we could make the day work to our benefit."

"I'm listening."

"What if we include Shawn in our day?"

"And why would we do that?"

"Even though this California visit is supposed to be for us, plainly, it isn't. So let's use it to our advantage. ...One of those keep-your-friends-close-and-your-enemies-closer things. Do you think he'll go for it?"

"Sure he will. He's a celebrity-monger. He wants what you have Hank, even though he doesn't know what that is."

"Ok then! You shower and I'll put things into play on my end. I know just what to do."

While Jocy gets ready, I make a few phone calls to my friends in high and fun places. They'll meet me at the book signing. Shawn will be easily enticed to be with them, leaving Jocy and me alone.

Things moved along well. Shawn agreed to meet Jocy at Barnes and Nobel, but I arranged for his attention to be distracted by two of my friends. These friends happened to be Hollywood producers. Shawn would know these fellows by both their names and appearance.

Sure enough, everything was moving along perfectly. Just as I was to begin the book signing, I noticed my friends walking towards me, and I gestured for Shawn to come my way.

"Shawn, step over here a sec, I'd like to introduce you to two of my special friends, Steven Sterling and Rod Sturgeon."

"Oh no intro is necessary, Hank," Shawn said almost too eagerly. "I've admired these two gentlemen for a long time."

Shawn eagerly shook both their hands and after pleasantries were extended, my friends graciously invited him to a lunch meeting.

Shawn, not being an idiot, was a little cautious as to why the 'fast invitation' by such well known producers, who didn't know him from Adam. So, I told him the truth.

"Shawn, let's be honest; I know you want to know more about me and my money. Here's your chance. The three of us have long standing partnerships. They have my permission to answer any questions you have, as long at it falls within their judgment to do so. Plus Shawn, it's a win-win. You get them and I get Jocy for the afternoon." And with that, Shawn and my eyes locked with each other. It was a standoff, but one he couldn't stand down from. He would go with them, and Jocy would go with me. And that's the way it would be.

Agreeing as if almost wanting to compliment my cleverness, but he wouldn't let himself. He had a job to do, and it was going to have to be ok that he enjoy part of it.

The three of them went to the café next door while Jocy got to see me in action. The book signing was a success by all standards. Jack would be happy.

With both the book signing and Shawn out of the way, it was time for Jocy and me to enjoy the rest of our time. Just as we exited the bookstore, Jocy's cell phone buzzed. It was the familiar buzz that usually takes me out of hearing range. I knew this was to be a private conservation.

Our eyes met. She knew I understood. I motioned that I would meet her at the car.

THIRTY

Jocy slips her phone back in her pocket and moves towards me and the waiting car. "Well, that was interesting."

"Interesting, good?"

"…Maybe. Shawn informed our mutual parties of his meeting with your producers. Seems they want him to see how this goes. He'll be staying a few days."

As she tells me this, I can't help but smile.

"Hank, did you set this up?"

"Well, Jocy, I told you I knew just want to do. And I think you'll find our producer friends will be taking Shawn on location, away from us for a day or two."

"That was certainly clever!"

"Yes, I thought so. Now we can get back to you and me."

"That sounds great, but you do know that they are expecting some type of information about your wealth to come out of our time together here. They think there is more to you than entertainment investments. They want more—do you have something more, Hank?"

And with that question I took Jocy's hands and looked her squarely in the face. "Jocy, as much as I want to see where this is going—you and me, I mean—don't you think they would be suspicious? I mean, if only after a few days of knowing you, I were to spill all of what they think are my secrets?"

"Yes, of course you are right. I just feel the pressure some-times. I'm sorry I pushed."

"No need to apologize. At some point soon, I'll give you something to wet their appetites a bit. In the meantime, I have my own appetite. I'm starving! Let's grab a late lunch. There's a great café 'round the corner."

THIRTY ONE

While we're sitting across from one another's Caesar salads, I get a call from Jack. Jocy watches my face as I listen attentively.

"Hank, you need to get back to New York. There's a situation developing. Can you be back by three p.m. tomorrow?"

I understood the *three p.m.* reference. This meant that Jack, Sam and I would be meeting at our library gateway. I wasn't ready to discuss any of this with Jocy.

"Jocy, something came up with my contract involving other publishers who are fighting Jack for my book. I need to be there in person to help him sort this out."

It wasn't quite the truth, but it was enough for Jocy to understand the importance of getting back to New York, cutting our time together short. Plus giving her too much information could be detrimental to her safety.

THIRTY TWO

We stopped in Nevada on the way back to Virginia. I was doing some research on my next book, 'Gems of Antiquity'. The subject matter was precious stones.

Jocy found the topic interesting and was eager to assist with research. Plus, we both knew, it would give us more time together in what would seem to others as legitimate work.

Then something unexpected showed up as Jocy was researching some deeds to some obscure mines.

"Hank, take a look at this," she said. "This is a familiar name to me."

As I glanced over her shoulder with the scent of Channel #5 caressing my face, Jocy pointed with her pen to this corporate name: 'Stiletto'. She leaned back into me. I felt a wonderful charge.

I had yet to speak, when Jocy's cell rang. I watched her face as she stepped away and her eyes looked to the floor. She lowered her phone, tucked it in her pocket.

Silence.

There was something she wanted to tell me, but couldn't. I could tell by the way she looked away. This wasn't good. And she couldn't tell me.

"Hank, do you mind if we just step away from the research for today, and just enjoy one another?"

I was concerned about her change in mood. She had become anxious, but of course I welcomed her invitation to just enjoy the day. "Sure Jocy. Jack keeps a corporate penthouse suite at the Bellagio in Las Vegas. Are you comfortable with that?"

"Am I comfortable staying at one of the most famous, luxurious, extravagant hotels in the world, with a very handsome man in tow? Let me take a millisecond to think." She smiled. "Of course! This will be a wonderful change of scenery for me."

There was something hidden in what she was saying, but I went along and didn't pressure her. I hoped she would confide in me as she relaxed a bit. She seemed to be preoccupied, but disguising it pretty well.

Jocy remained quiet on our ride back into town from the dessert, but her eyes and face lit up as we hit the Vegas Strip. Las Vegas was full of everything and anything that could take your mind away from your concerns of the day. It seemed this is what Jocy needed most.

Checking in, Jocy noticed that the staff seemed to know me. "Welcome back Mr. Ramsan." and "Hello, Hank, Great to see you!" High fives came from all levels of the staff.

"You are quite popular, Hank," Jocy observed. "Come here often?"

"Well, Jocy, I've been researching my book, and this is a Wade Publishing hotel. Jack's one of the investors. So they simply know me from frequency, not famously. Plus this hotel is known for its discretion. Most of the higher-end Vegas hotels operate under a veil of sorts. You know the one, 'What happens in Vegas, stays in Vegas!'"

"Yes, Hank and now some other things are beginning to make sense."

"Like what things, Jocy?"

"...Things like I can't tell you about, not yet, anyway."

I sensed her getting tense again, so I left it alone. Even though I was eager to find out more, I didn't want to talk about business. I wanted this to be about us. I sensed the same from her.

THIRTY THREE

Aroma of fresh flowers filled the room as the bellman opened the wide doors that led into the sumptuous suite.

A second bellhop near Jocy pretended to shake her hand in greeting. Immediately, she flinched and pulled away.

"Young man," I said rather hastily. "Here's your tip. Thank you very much." I wanted him out of the room fast.

Once the door was securely closed, I turned to her. "Jocy, what happened? What did you see?"

"All I can tell you, Hank, is that bellhop had a familiar tattoo on his wrist. And he wanted me to see it."

"Are you in danger, Jocy?"

"No, I don't think so. They just wanted me to know I needed to behave myself."

"Behave yourself in regard to what?"

"Hank, in regard to why I am really here with you. I cannot divulge much more than that."

"...Ok, that. Well, maybe I can give you some information that will keep them satisfied for a while. Until then, how 'bout we hit the strip?" Celine Dion and Brittany Spears, both have great shows, as well as Cirque Du Soleil is hosted in the Bellagio."

She said, "If it's all the same to you, can we just stay in? Maybe enjoy a wonderful meal, and then sit out on the balcony and take in the night from here?"

"Sure, that sounds great to me. Let's unpack and take a look at the room service menu."

We agreed on Surf and Turf with Caesar Salads. I ordered Dom Perignon and Madria Sangria.

"Jocy, I know you don't drink much, as neither do I, but on this occasion, I have a special mixture of champagne and sangria. It's smooth, fruity, light and it takes the edge off."

A knock on the door announced our dinner and drinks. I answered it, so that there wouldn't be another incident of discomfort for Jocy.

Pushing the cart to the balcony where Jocy was already seated, I poured our mixture and handed her a glass.

"Hank this is delicious! What is this mixture of yours called?"

"DomMaddy"

"DomMaddy? Why DomMaddy?"

"Dom for the Champaign and Maddy is a secret that I'll share with you at another time."

"Is Maddy an old girlfriend? I'm sure you've had many?"

"I'll take that as a compliment Jocy, but no, Maddy has nothing to do with any old girlfriends. But the name does have something to do with my being Privately Famous. And there you go, there's something you can pass along to your *friends*."

THIRTY FOUR

Las Vegas nights could be warm and cool at the same time. The DomMaddy was helping Jocy to relax, and she opened up a bit more about her past. She began telling the story of her rise to success in the art world, but wouldn't say much more than that. She wasn't willing to talk about her family.

She wanted to know more about me and what made me tick. The questions about the wealth had ceased to be part of our conversation. Genuine interest and care were showing themselves more often.

Jocy placed her drink on the ledge of the balcony and took my hand. Kissing me on my cheek, she led me back into the suite and into the bedroom. She excused herself to the dressing room by saying, "Don't move. I'll be right back."

Tossing off my shoes, glancing towards the dressing room door opening; there she was, waiting, wanting me. I walked towards her and noticed the soft thin t-shirt she was wearing. "I've seen this before, haven't I?"

"Yes, Hank, it's the one I was wearing on our first night together."

I put my arms around her and became immediately aware of her beautiful full round breasts leaning into my chest. We both began moving our hands up one another's clothes. Jocy was unbuttoning my shirt as my hands were caressing her breasts.

The kisses were deep and breathtaking. I was lost in her. I was lost in her more than I had ever been lost before or since.

My 'waiting in the weeds' moment was front and center. Nothing in my imagination could have matched the melting and melding of her skin on mine.

The night became a gentle but passionate blur, blending into the space as one unforgettable image. I was mesmerized in her glow, her warmth, her affection, her sensual touch. What was it about this girl that captivated me so? It didn't matter. I was in deep. Time stopped, the moment was still. It was like she knew my body the way she knew the back of her own hand.

The world could have ended that night and I wouldn't have known or cared. That night would be forever burned into my mind.

THIRTY FIVE

My internal clock told me it was morning, although the room was dark due to the thick curtains still drawn. I turned over in the large king size bed thinking I would touch Jocy and wake her. I reached for her. She wasn't there. Something wasn't right. I could feel it.

A sealed envelope with *Hank* written on it lay on the pillow where Jocy once slept. My hand was trembling a bit. That has never happened before.

Hand written prose on the Bellagio stationary filled my eyes along with an ache in my chest. The words could have been written by Casanova to Jane Austen. They had the impact of enchantment, sensual affection and ended in the One Love, Lost.

The flow of her words told me I was as much her one, as she mine. Ending with, "I Love You Hank, Jocy."

And then almost as an afterthought, but not wanting to spoil the message of the prose, there was a second page:

Hank, thank you for all of our time out west. It was so wonderful being with you. You fill in all the spaces of my heart. Don't try to find me. Jocy.

That was it. The Letter, which tore at my heartstrings and the knowledge that she was gone. Gone?

Just like that? How could that be? No explanation, just gone.

THIRTY SIX

After exhausting all efforts within the hotel to find out if anyone had seen her leave, and turning up nothing, I called Jack.

"Jack, she disappeared. She's gone. We had an incredible time, a beautiful night. The only reminder is a beautiful prose she wrote to me. At the end she tells me not to try and find her. Jack … no explanation. …Just gone. My heart is ripped."

I held back the tears that were choking up my throat. I was a man, not prone to emotion of this nature, which made it all the more agonizing. I'd never felt this way about anyone.

Jack said he'd get Sam on it, but he asked me a few questions first.

"Hank, you went to Las Vegas and visited some mines in the desert, right?"

"Yes, we were doing research on that book that's up for auction."

"Ah … hmm, yes, I see it now."

"You see what, Jack."

"You touched on a major nerve with your research, which normally wouldn't cause any flack, except this was *you* Hank Ramsan. You're known for specific themes, and then add Jocy to the mix. Yes, I can see some of the surface of this. We'll talk more when you get back to New York, not on the phone."

"…Very well."

"Not to add to your misery, Hank, but remember you have to make an appearance in Virginia at the book festival."

"I've not forgotten Jack. I'll be there on time."

Jumping into the shower, I noticed that everything of Jocy's was gone. Everything except that thin sexy t-shirt from our only two nights together. Holding it to my face, it smelled of her. I knew she left it behind for me.

Hope against hope, I was still trying to turn up any leads that would tell me what happened to her, and where she went. Was she safe?

The hotel wasn't any help. They wouldn't let me see the security tapes without authorization. I kept pushing, finally some burly fellow told me to back off and that there had been a problem with the AV system on that particular day, and "there was nothing on any of the tapes."

Yeah sure, I thought to myself.

There was no use contacting the police. I was sure someone owned them, plus there was no evidence of foul play. They might just assume she simply left me. But I knew better. At least that's what I told myself.

Time was short. Getting to the airport, on to Virginia for the conference, then to New York. There was more going on than I could control at this point. I needed to get back to New York and get my head on straight.

THIRTY SEVEN

It was also possible that my trying to find her might jeopardize her safety even more. Creative means needed to be implemented, if in fact I was to ever see her again. Being creative was my thing, plus it would keep me focused and on track.

Even though Jocy appeared to have simply left, I was sure, or at least I told myself that it wasn't of her free will. I was glad however, that I had not disclosed any of my wealth secrets as it would have put many more than just Jocy at risk. Plus it would have hampered my overall plan for wealth accumulation for the masses.

It was time for me to implement some of the methods which were the basis of my wealth, while keeping me 'Privately Famous'. Quite possibly, these same methods would lead me back to Jocy.

What I did not want was for my actions to affect her adversely. Whatever I did next, if anything, it would only be known to me, Jack and Sam.

The Wade Jet was waiting for me on the runway. Settling back into the leather seats I began reflecting on the past few days.

Jocy and I had a wonderful time together. We were becoming close, almost intimate. Then she was gone. Just Gone!

I didn't know if she was in danger or if she had known all along about her abrupt exit. Maybe it was her job to tangle with my heart strings. But that letter she left. My heart will ache for awhile.

My main reason for wanting to go to Virginia and appear on the panel was to spend more time with Jocy. But now I would simply appear, be professional and inspiring, and then immediately fly back to New York to meet Jack and Sam.

Suddenly it dawned on me: What about Shawn? I'd forgotten all about him. The last I knew, he was being entertained by my producer friends. Where was he now, and did he have anything to do with Jocy's disappearance?

My thoughts were interrupted by the pilot over the intercom and the usual buckle-up message. Landing was smooth and I was met by one of the organizers of the book fair. We exchanged pleasantries during the ride into Charlottesville. I was preoccupied with the previous days, so was not overly talkative.

Shifting my focus to the book fair panel needed to take precedent for the moment. This would be important for me, Wade World Wide Publishing, and the Consortium.

My presentation was clear and inspiring. All writers there envied my success. What they didn't know was that they could implement the same things I had done, easily, without all the hard work and effort that is usually preached as the only way to success in writing.

I knew a better way and used it efficiently. But the timing was off for me to share it. Or maybe now was the perfect time. I wasn't sure.

If I had been the bait for Jocy to produce, and she was unsuccessful and disappeared, what would happen if I did share my secrets of becoming 'Privately Famous'?

THIRTY EIGHT

Having a half hour remaining on flight back to New York, I called one of my producer friends in LA to find out about Shawn.

As it turned out, Shawn abruptly exited their time together.

"Hank, he got a phone call while we were en route to Universal. He apologized for his abruptness, thanked us for our time, 'an emergency' was all he said."

His leaving their meeting happened around the same time as our Las Vegas visit.

I thanked my friends for providing the diversion for Shawn.

"Anytime, Hank! And we have first option on Privately Famous, right?"

"Of Course it goes without saying … always!"

It didn't really matter about Shawn. He was just a pawn in the overall scheme of things, whatever those schemes were.

Sam met me at the Wade Hanger. As we drove to our three p.m. meeting he had some interesting news.

"Hank, I had an art dealer friend try to contact Jocy for one of his paintings, to see if anything would turn up. He was told she was unavailable and would be out of the country for an unspecified amount of time. He pressed a bit more. 'I have an important client with a substantial interest in a famous painting. Jocy is the only one he trusts to deal with. Can you somehow put me in touch with her?'"

"...And?" I was sure I wouldn't like where this was going. Something was really wrong.

"The answer he was given was cryptic. He was told that Jocy decided to retire from the art world and her gallery, and that her company would be under new ownership. My friend was told someone would follow up with him soon."

"What do you think this means?"

"Hank, let's wait to see what Jack has to say."

"Sounds good, Sam. Mind hitting that Starbucks drive-thru before we get into the City?"

"Of course, there's one just ahead."

I was quiet on the way in. Sam and I, being friends forever are quite comfortable with silence during a car ride.

Thirty minutes later, coffee in hand, two for me, one each for Sam and Jack, we drove underground to Jack's offices. Employees of Wade Publishing could park underground, but were unaware of the hidden pathway, which connected Jack's office, my loft and The Library.

Reaching his hand out, Jack said, "Right on time, gentlemen. Thanks for the coffee, Hank." Pulling our chairs up to the strong, wide, deep mahogany table, he added, "Sam filled you in, right?"

"Yes. Do you have anything more on your end?"

"There's no sign of Jocy or Shawn, Hank. I know she's important to you, as well as our overall mission. Maybe there's something you can do to incorporate both?"

"Both... Meaning what exactly?"

"Somehow, Hank your skills have irritated those who control the purse strings. Jocy was used to try and get information, but from what you've said, you didn't give away much."

"We had so little time together."

Jack took a long sip of coffee. "We have to assume she is being held against her will, and we have to hope she is still alive. But Hank, I know you began to care for her, and to trust her. But what if that was her job? Until we know for sure, we have to be careful. Otherwise, all we have done to assist in the world changes will be for nothing."

"Of course you're right, Jack." I agreed. "And I had been thinking along the same lines. I have an idea that if it works, it could work in our favor in many ways. And if it doesn't, we will have unleashed a monster."

"Ok, Hank, Sam and I are all ears."

I had the attention and loyalty of my two best friends. We all could lose our lives, and those we loved, if my plan didn't work. I watched their faces as I began.

I slowly became aware that I was holding the pineapple-shaped golden crystal in my right hand. Thoughts were shaping in my head. "...What if I outline the keys to my becoming rich and wealthy, while remaining Privately Famous? It might be the thing that would flush these Stiletto characters out into the open, expose them; which could in turn add to the ease of energetic wealth creation for the masses."

"That just might work, Hank. They wouldn't want the world to know what you know, and be able to implement it successfully. They may come after you." Jack took another long sip of coffee. "Are you ready for that?"

"Of course I am. We've reached the place where it's time. Meeting Jocy put us in the same world as the Stiletto. This will allow us to expose them, and rid the control they have over the world's money."

"Perhaps," Jack agreed.

"We know there are no accidents," I continued. "Jocy became a pleasant surprise, maybe a pawn used by both sides, depending on the truth of her loyalty. None the less, now we know more than we did."

"Ok, Hank," Jack agreed. "Sam and I are in, of course. So what's the plan, and how do you want us to help?"

THIRTY NINE

I proceeded to introduce an idea to Jack and Sam. "What if we establish another group of sorts? This group may only be joined by invitation. …Invitation, of which, we control for our own agenda. This agenda would be known only to the three of us."

Jack was a bit leery, "You mean in addition to the Consortium group? Won't that confuse things?"

"Yes and No. Yes, in addition to the Arts and Writers group, but No, it won't confuse things as this group will be only by invitation to the elite in the financial world. The main intent of setting up this group is to flush out the conspirators. It will not be an open or promoted group."

"Go on," Jack said.

"The name of the group: 'The Privately Famous Trust'. The word *trust* carries several meanings, depending upon one's perspective. For our purposes, the word *trust* implies our trust in the hidden aspect that only we know. *Trust*, for others implies a financial implement used for monetary protections. Others still define trust as a large company."

"Ok. I get it," Jack said. "We purposely leak information about the trust, and we see who shows up to try and secure an invitation."

"Yes, exactly, and here's the thing. If we really wanted to find Jocy, we could. Disappearing without a trace these days is almost impossible. And what if she doesn't want to be found?

What if she was manipulating me in some way? I do have to consider that possibility. As much as I wanted to trust her, for as much as I wanted her to be the one, something was a bit 'off.'"

"And Hank," Jack agreed, "if she was using you, possibly setting up the *Privately Famous Trust* would bring us more information about Jocy, and her role."

"Yes, as you can see, I'm still a bit caught up in it. But I'll get over it for the sake of the larger picture. Besides, the only thing I had at the end of it was a wonderful prose and then the note, 'It's Over.' Her 'it's over' note was telling me that the prose was not original, she had copied it. And that her job was complete and that whatever I thought we had was a 'social engineering' of sorts."

"But Hank, if all of that were true, why would she go to the trouble of explaining it?"

"I really don't know Jack. I was blindsided and my heart was smashed, but still a part of me hopes that there was something there."

"For now, I have to compartmentalize my thoughts and efforts. It's time to flush out the underbelly of the darker side of wealth. The organization that's been giving the rich and wealthy a bad reputation. This is to be the moment of: 'There are things that are done in the dark, that are done in the Light.'"

Sam, who is normally quiet, questioned 'the after'. "Hank what happens to this Privately Famous Group, to those that are innocent after we hopefully flush out the connections to the underworld? We don't want them to feel used."

"Great question, Sam. My thinking is that this PFT group would be used as an oversight committee for the Arts and Writers Consortium. That way, we wouldn't be in the position to ever be accused of showing favoritism to any one party. There would be other wise counsel involved with this second group."

Both Sam and Jack nodded in agreement, as we moved on to the task of setting up the meeting.

FORTY

Jack took care of designing and sending out the invitations to *The Privately Famous Trust*. Only those on Jack's media list would be receiving them. The word would pass like gossip and anyone that wanted to be there, but was not invited, would find a way to secure an invite. It's simply how these things work, and we all knew it.

The invitations were eloquently designed. Gold Laced envelopes and parchment Inserts. The only words on the parchment were, 'The Privately Famous Trust / RSVP / Wade Worldwide Publishing. Nine seats available.'

These nine seats would have to be purchased. Jack, Sam and I knew that in this way, at least one of the seats would be owned by those attempting to make a deception of wealth accumulation.

Within three days of the invitations being sent, all nine slots were purchased.

The first PFT meeting was set. The group would gather in the Wade conference room.

Prior to the meeting of some of the wealthiest people on the planet, I would have to design and outline what I was going to say. I had to decide what I would give, and what I would hold back.

The whole purpose of setting up the PFT was to give enough information to show how easy it would be for the masses to accumulate financial wealth. Holding back the one aspect which would change the balance of the world's finances as we knew it, would be on me.

Jack, Sam and I knew that the puzzle piece I was holding back until the right time was the exact piece that someone was attempting to procure, use for themselves, then hide from the ones we intended to help worldwide.

I had to be clear and concise, while making the unbelievable, believable. It was time to sell the magic.

FORTY ONE

The morning of the Privately Famous Trust presentation arrived. Ten a.m. promptly, as is usual with successful business types, all a bit early. Four women, five men. All seated around the mahogany conference table. Water, coffee, juice at the ready.

I began with a brief introduction:

"Welcome! We all prefer concise information, so I'll begin with a short background."

"Having a long-standing interest and curiosity about the esoteric side of life, I knew there were other levels, other understandings related to higher knowledge. It's been my lifelong intent to learn of these things and translate them through my writing. Just as important would be my ability to translate the higher knowledge in new ways, in which the masses could easily implement the information to their own benefit as well as all others. The higher intention would automatically happen."

Looking around the room, I was watchful of the interest level as well as any signs that I might be boring anyone. So far, so good. All were attentive and respectful. Again, a trait of highly successful men and women. I was in good company.

Continuing: "I knew I was born to this. Thus began my studies and research into the Himalayan Masters as well as what we have come to call The Ancients."

"I've kept most of my understandings to myself, except for two of my trusted confidants. Applying these understandings to my own life has allowed me to become Privately Famous. By that I mean, I have all the material wants and needs that I could ever desire, plus more. I've been able to accomplish this through my writing, while remaining somewhat unknown. This has been my intent all along. I was never interested in fame or celebrity, although I have studied those who have chosen those lifestyles, if only to learn something from them."

A hand lifted as in a question. It was from one of the other more famous billionaires, whom shall remain nameless out of respect for the individual, as well as for the overall reason for the meeting.

"Hank, I've also studied you for a long time and have been aware of your success and your ability to remain under the radar, so to speak. This is why I am most interested in why we've been brought here. I know you must have something of grand importance on your mind, or you would not have sent out the lavish invitations to a group of this stature."

"Yes. Thank you, Harvey, (not his real name). Thank you for answering the invite and becoming a part of this." I drew a deep breath. "So, here it is: Please indulge me a bit further on some personal history, as it will be crucial to your understanding."

FORTY TWO

"At a young age I discovered, or really I was given a powerful success stone. We've all seen movies about magic stones and read books. And most of the time they were presented as fiction. This is not fiction."

All eyes were on me as they listened intently.

"I was given a crystal citrine in the shape of a pineapple. As you may know, the pineapple has long been a symbol of opulence, wealth and prosperity."

From another of the attendees came, "Yes, Hank, I too am aware of the power of certain crystals. These were first introduced as far as we know by those of Atlantis. And of course some believe in the Atlantis story and others do not."

"Yes, you are correct of course. There is much knowledge buried for those of us seeking it. I'm glad to know you also have been one. I was told that whoever was in possession of this stone had only to trust it as Aladdin would trust his Magic Lamp. It was with this stone and my understanding of the working of higher law that was needed to build my wealth."

What I did not tell this group is that there was a formula in using the stone. However, the formula brings forth wealth without the need for the stone. It was my plan to introduce the stone, knowing that there would be those who would try to take it from me.

"Ladies and Gentlemen, the purpose of The Privately Famous Trust is to pass along the following, by whatever methods we feel led to introduce to the masses: How to accumulate wealth in the easiest and most peaceful ways and means."

After a pause to let that sink in, I continued: "You in this room, you did not achieve your status without a great deal of compassion for your fellow man. It is my desire that you use your wisdom along with your compassion to introduce the formula I'm about to pass out to you." (This formula is vastly unique from the formula required for the stone, but I didn't tell this group, that.)

I could see the anticipation in their faces as I began passing out the gold folders containing the formula.

FORTY THREE

Below is that actual formula I gave in written form to those nine individuals seated in the conference room.

The Privately Famous Formula

A. There are Two Attentions.

The Power is in The Second Attention. It is with the Second Attention that we understand why no physical action is required. (Learn and Practice what this is.)

B. There are Two Types of Imagination.

(Learn and Understand The Two Types)

C. Learn The Ancient Power, Higher Law Techniques in How to Exactly Use The Light for Desire Fulfillment.

Caution: If we do not believe that this level of power is available to us and understand how to use it, then it will not work for us.

A Quotation Which Best Serves The Caution:

'The Absolute prerequisite for the Acquisition and Manifestation of Intuitive Knowledge and Direct Power is the Awareness That Such Knowledge and Power are Available.' (Loc 468 The Golden Crown-Manuscript of The Great Master Kalika-Khenmetator, circa 1370 BC)

FORTY FOUR

"Are there any questions regarding this meeting or the formula itself?"

"Yes, I have one."

"Great, Rich, what is it?"

"What is next after this meeting? We have this formula, we have a basic understanding of why you called this particular group together. But what's next? Do we get back together, report in or what?"

"Rich, I've not set an agenda for *next*. I know that those of you who take the idea of this Trust, its intent, along with the formula, will see it all take on a life of its own. I don't want to try and direct it. You all are great ambassadors of your chosen fields. You will know what to do, when to do it and whom to do it with."

"Ok then, I'm good. I've got another meeting. Are we done here Hank?"

"Yes, and thank you all for coming."

I watched them leave, still not knowing for sure which one if any of them was someone who would show their hand.

What I did not tell the group was that there are techniques that only those using their higher mind can access and understand. The Intellectual and Lower mind are not in tune with these higher methods. Which means, the intent to steal the crystal, which I felt was sure to happen, would simply nullify its power to that user. I knew that they would not.

It would take more than belief. The user of the formula would need to come to know that the power exists for everyone. Only through the practice, knowledge and understanding would the results be opulence, wealth and fortune. It is exactly how I accomplished it.

FORTY FIVE

My cell rings just as I'm helping Savannah, (Jack's paralegal), tidy up the conference room. The number read, Unknown.

"Hello?"

I hear a familiar voice. It was Shawn.

"Hank, I'll ask politely first. I need for you to give me the stone."

"Well Shawn, nice to hear from you and thank you so much for being 'polite'. But how did you hear about the stone, you weren't at the meeting?"

"One of your attendees had a mic."

Jack, Sam and I agreed not to apply any security measures for this meeting, as in doing so, we might just uncover a microphone. If someone was there to try and sabotage the meeting in any way, we wanted to allow it to happen.

"I don't suppose you would let me know who was wearing it the mic? For old times sake?"

"Very funny, Hank, but no. When can we meet for you to give me the stone?"

"Right to the point again. What makes you think I'll just willingly hand it over? And besides, answer me this. What happened with Jocy?"

"She dumped you. That's what happened. Get over it. And you will willingly give me the stone, otherwise the markets that your precious Wade Publishing is involved in will take a sudden downturn and Jack Wade's empire with it."

I knew there was no way this would ever happen. But Shawn wouldn't have a clue about that.

I pretended to act like I knew I had no choice, and we made arrangements to meet.

The stone had done all it could do for me, which was why I could allow it to go. I had used the power of the stone while building my understandings of higher law and how to use it. In the wrong hands, which would be Shawn and his associates, it simply would be a pretty rock.

FORTY SIX

Shawn and I agreed to meet at the Wall Street Café'. I would be protected there. We sat in a back booth, coffee delivered. I started with what I wanted to know, and maybe it was me not wanting to face some brutal fact that Jocy really dumped me; or hope that something else was going on and that I had meant something to her.

"Shawn, I know you know something more of Jocy. She just couldn't have disappeared on me with no explanation."

"You want an explanation? Ok. Here it is. Jocy is part of our organization. She has been for some time. She's trained to do what she does. You are not the first to succumb to her beauty and charm. She used you for our purpose, which was to find out about how you achieved your level of wealth so easily. And now we know. I will have the stone and the formula."

"I want to hear this from Jocy," I said.

"She has a new project for us, and won't be returning to New York City. She used you. That's all it was to her."

Without another word, I handed him the stone.

EPILOGUE

Having first learned of higher law applications from fellow writer Susan James, it was she who first wanted to tell part of the story through *The Millionaire Maverick*. She did so with my full permission. I wasn't ready to tell the *Privately Famous* story at that time. Susan in *The Millionaire Maverick* wrote of my involvement with hidden secret agendas and of course, Jocy.

From Susan's description of *The Millionaire Maverick*:

> Adventure and suspense as one man challenges the powers that be to show all mankind how to obtain unlimited wealth.

> Susan James brings her popular User Friendly Physics theme to Hank Ramsan, The Millionaire Maverick.

> Hank made everyone Millionaires who learned to use his Magic Wall. This enraged the powers that controlled the world's banks because hidden secrets were revealed and lifestyles threatened, as the world's money systems crumbled.

> Only one person could save Hank from the peril he had created, only she didn't love him anymore.

Thanks for Reading Privately Famous!

Hank Ramsan

Details:

The Millionaire Maverick (by Susan James)

On Amazon: Paperback and Kindle

http://www.amazon.com/dp/B004XD3HLY

Susan James Amazon Page http://amzn.to/1UuIG2e

ABOUT THE AUTHOR

Hank Ramsan writes of higher law and its effect on our lives as we use it, consciously.

He is a product of his own study and knowledge and has soon to be released new titles which disclose the mysteries of manifestation and desire fulfillment.

Hank's home in cyberspace: http://www.PrivatelyFamous.com

And http://www.HankRamsan.com

Due to Hank's ongoing mission as it relates to the money band of the earth, his physical address is known only to his inner circle. He may be contacted through is fellow writer and business partner, Susan James/Vast Five

http://www.VastFive.com

http://www.SusanJames.org

http://www.SusanJamesBooks.com

http://www.SusanJamesSocks.com

http://www.SecretsInMySocks.com

RESOURCES:

Teachings of The Himalayan Masters
(Their Secret Knowledge and Practices)
M.G. Hawking and Heather Cantrell
Kilika-Khenmetaten (The Supreme Egyptian Adept)
M.G. Hawking and Heather Cantrell
Wisdom Masters Press

Sea Horse Sea Freight
seahorseseafreight.com